WINGS OF FIRE

THE OFFICIAL COLORING BOOK

BASED ON THE SERIES BY TUI T. SUTHERLAND
ART BY BRIANNA C. WALSH

SCHOLASTIC INC.

Illustrations by Brianna C. Walsh © 2022 Scholastic.
Characters © 2022 Tui T. Sutherland.
Border design © 2012 by Mike Schley

ISBN 978-1-338-81840-6

10 9 8 7 6 5 4 3 2 1   22 23 24 25 26
Printed in the U.S.A.   40
First printing 2022

FATESPEAKER

SUNNY

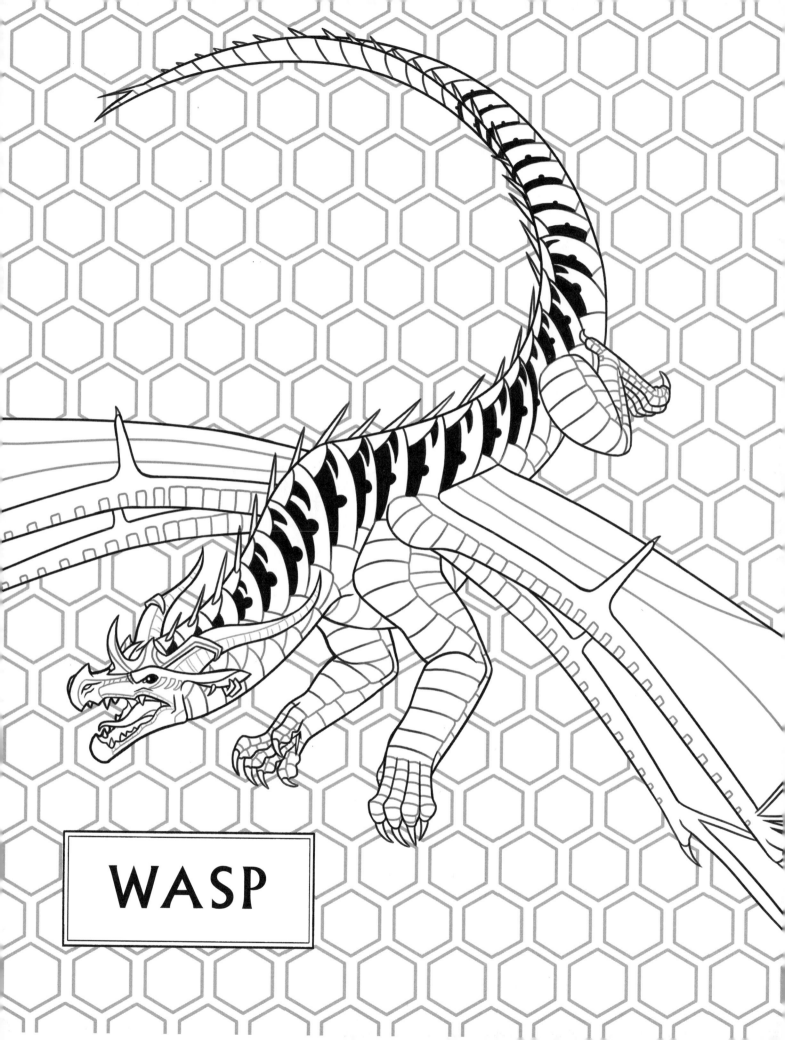

WASP

CORAL

MORROWSEER

FIERCETEETH

RUBY

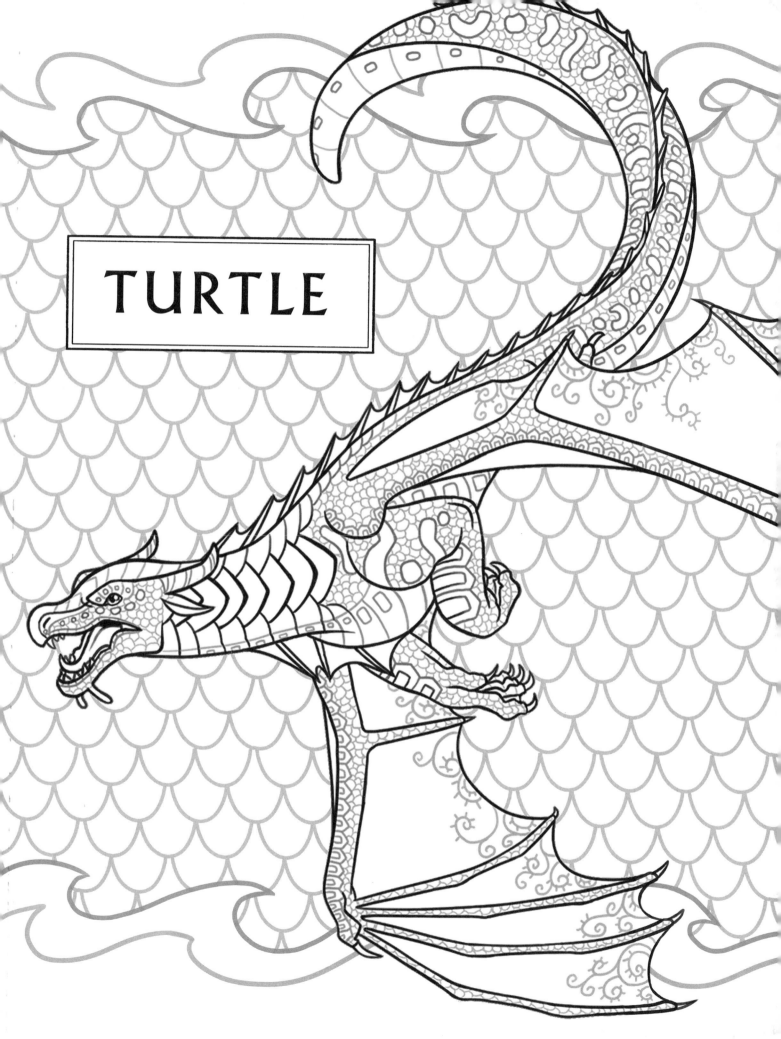

TURTLE

ICICLE

THORN

SCARLET

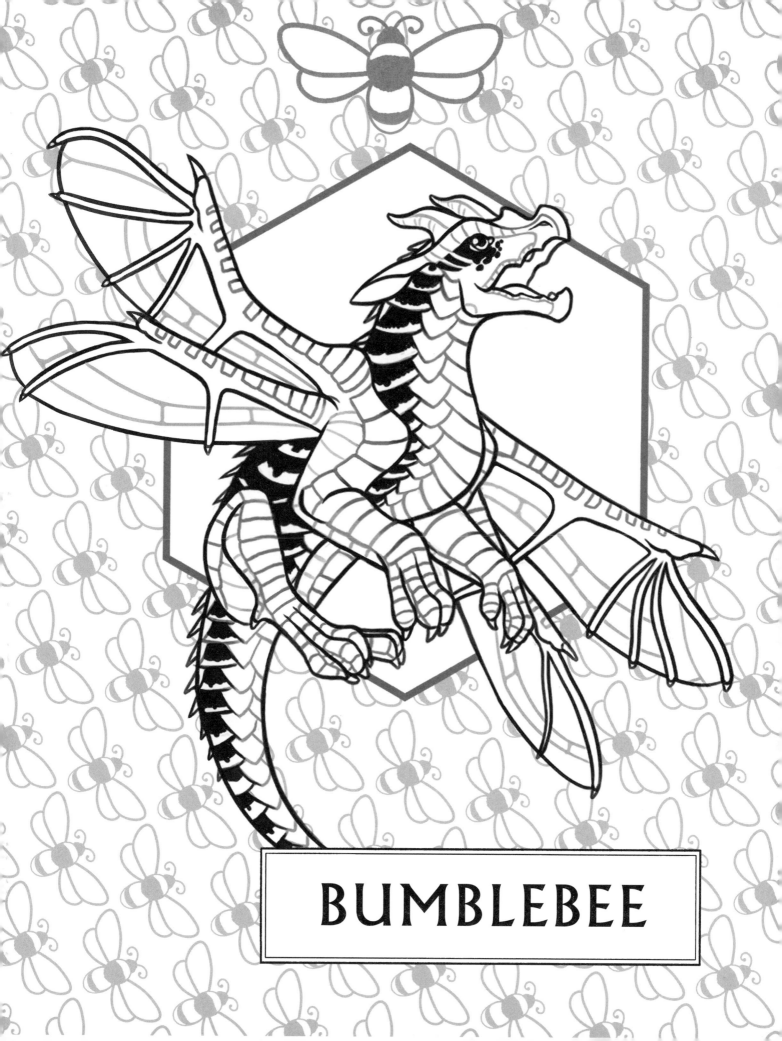

BUMBLEBEE

DARKSTALKER

SUNNY

FLAME

SNOWFALL

LYNX

WHITEOUT

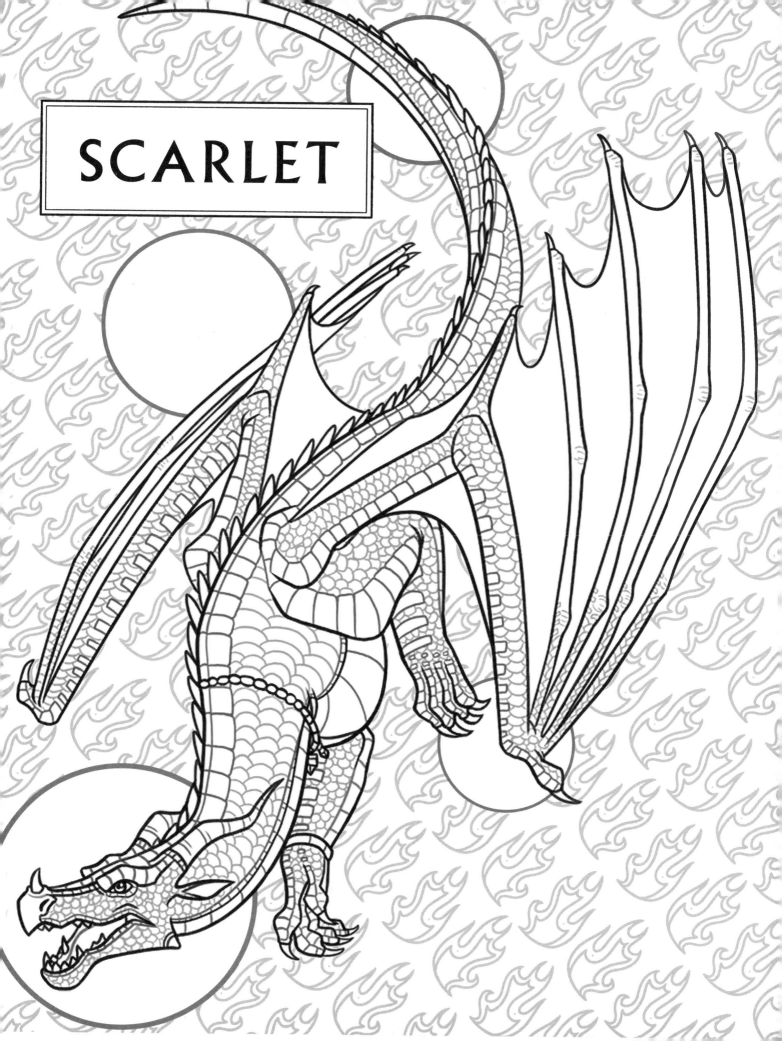

SCARLET

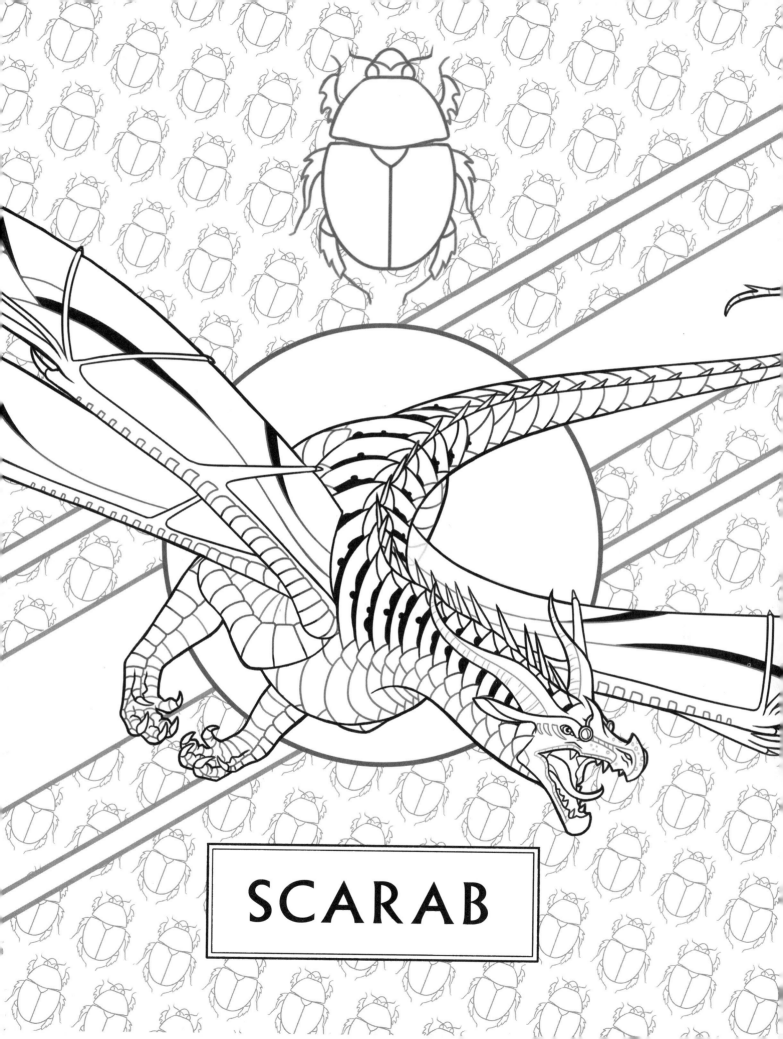

SCARAB

KESTREL

GLORY

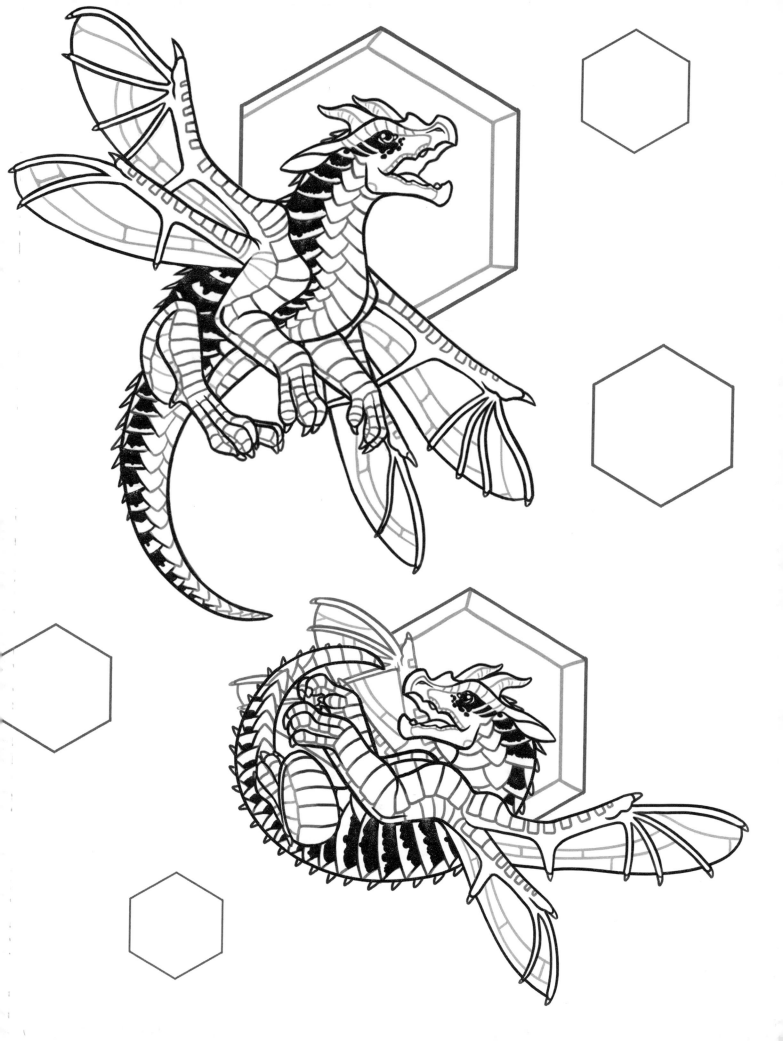

FATHOM

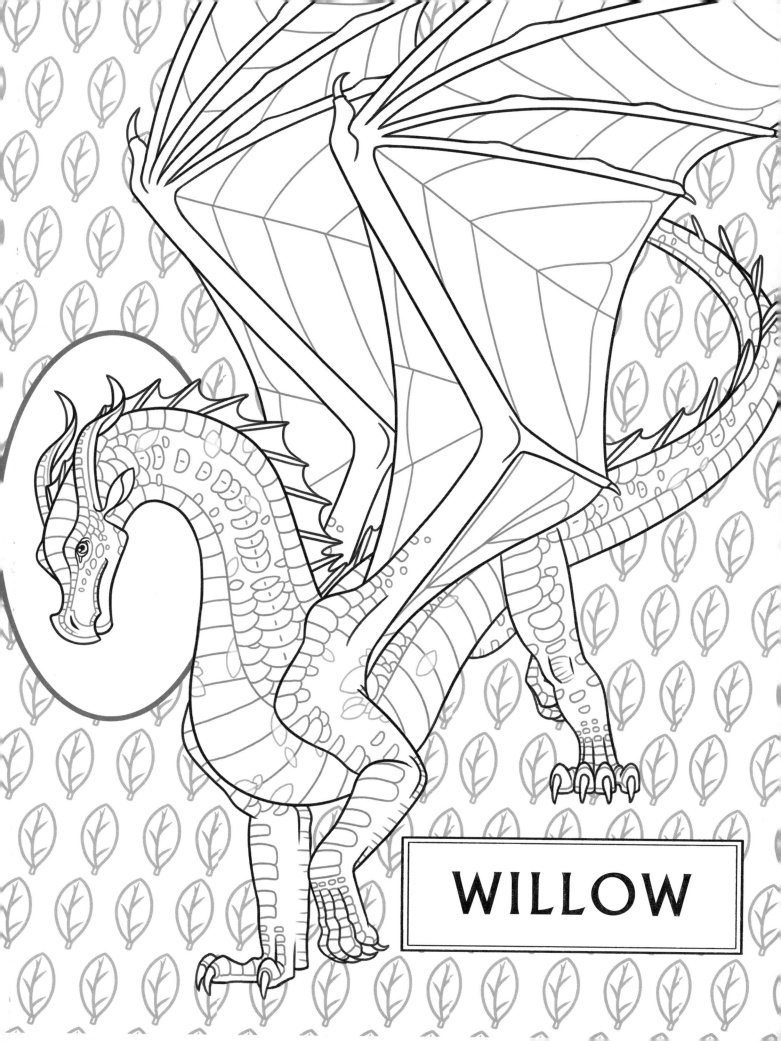

WILLOW

QIBLI

MOONWATCHER

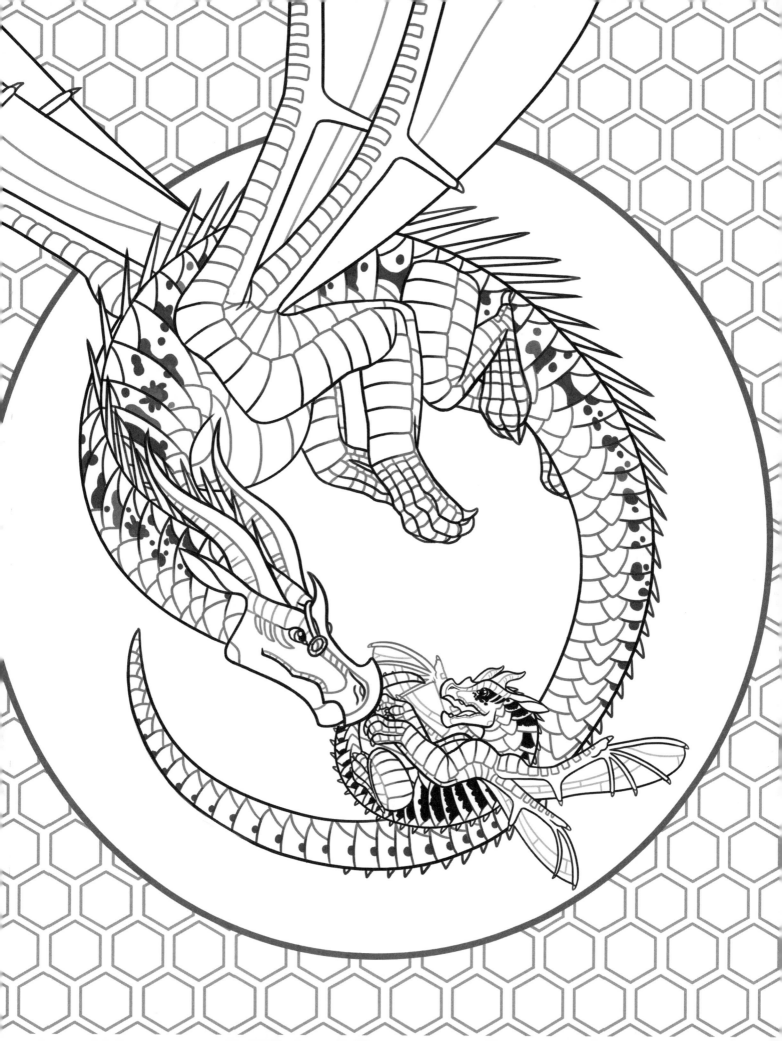

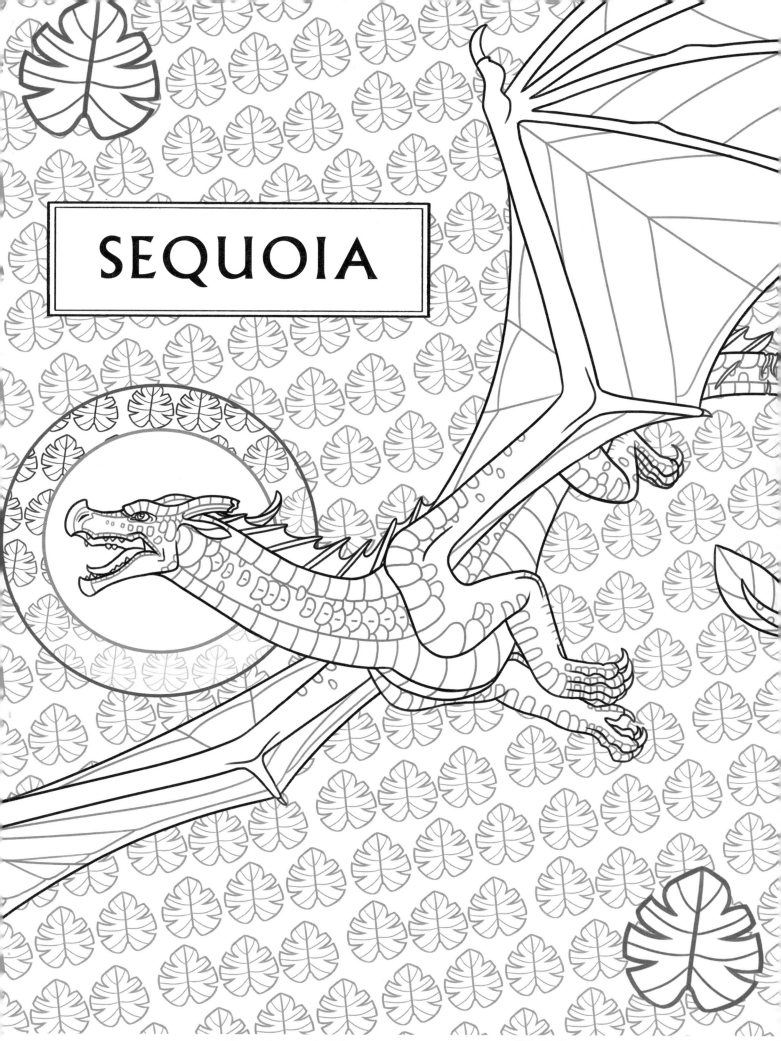

SEQUOIA

WILLOW

SUNDEW

FOESLAYER

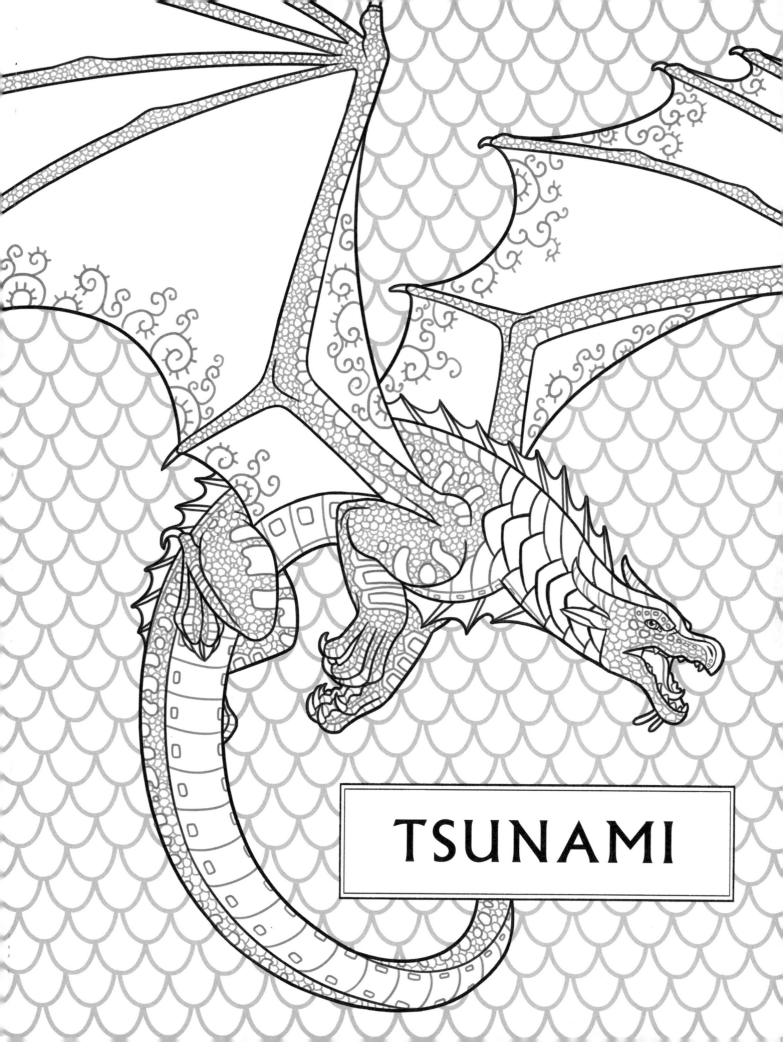

TSUNAMI

PEACEMAKER

SWORDTAIL

WINTER

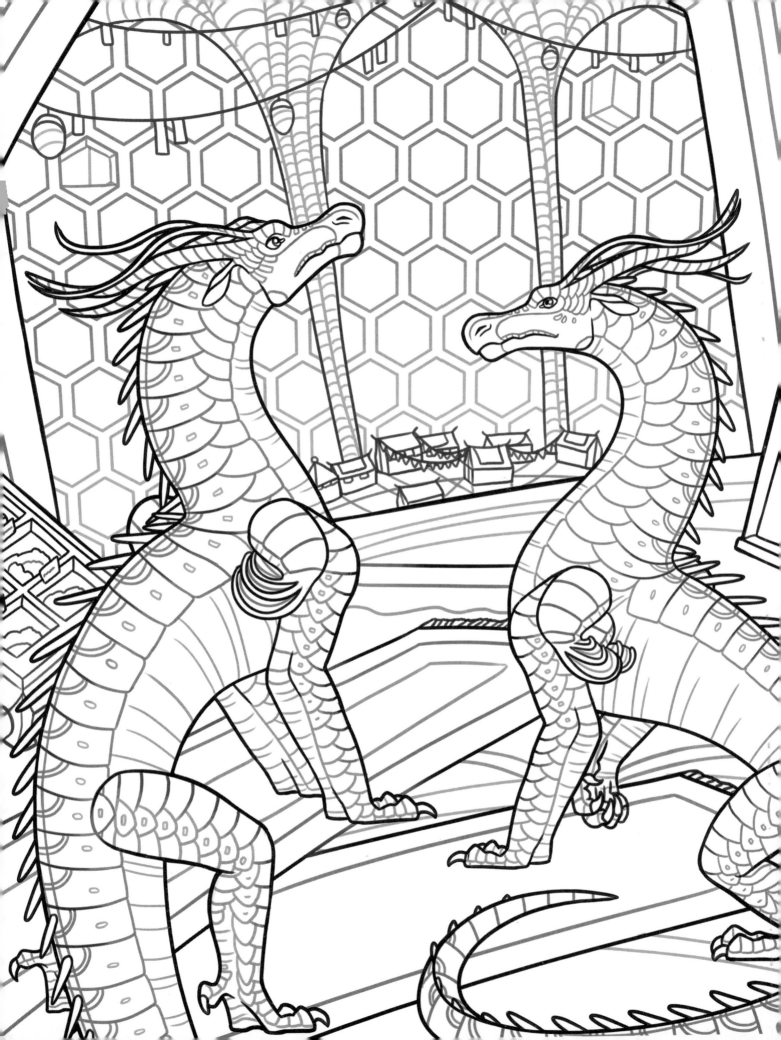

RIPTIDE

CLEARSIGHT

CLAY

UMBER

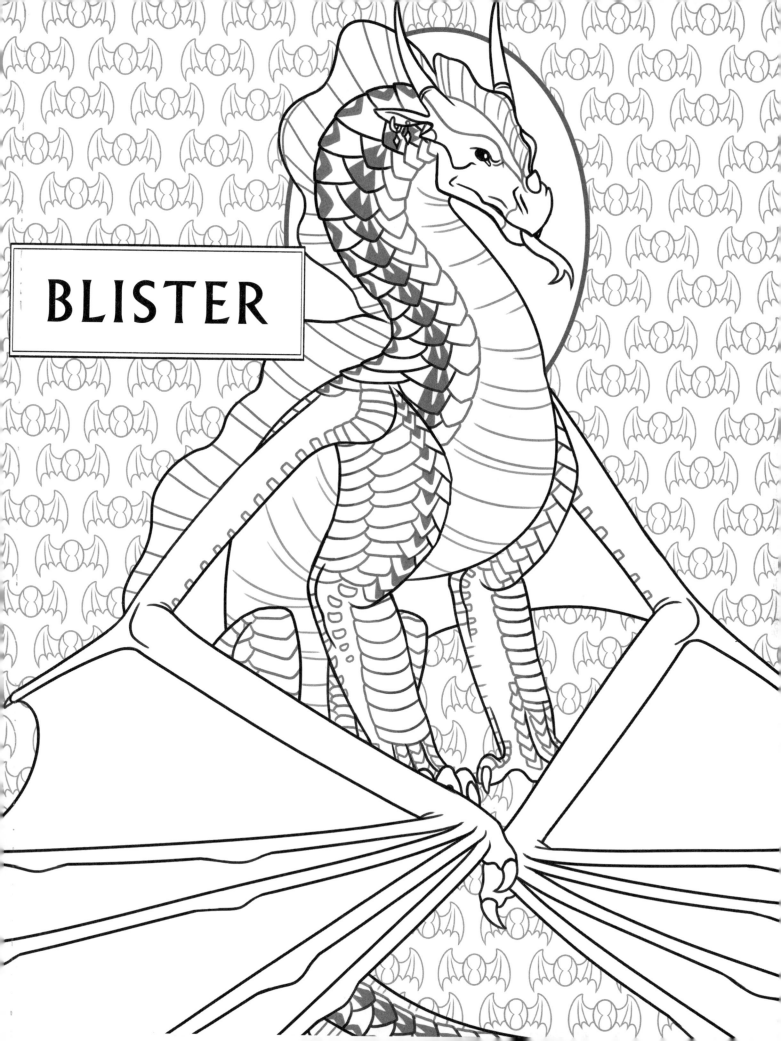

BLISTER

MONARCH

SKY & PERIL

BLUE